Unicorn Princesses
BLOOM'S BALL

The Unicorn Princesses series

Sunbeam's Shine

Flash's Dash

Bloom's Ball

Prism's Paint

Breeze's Blast

Moon's Dance

Firefly's Glow

Feather's Flight

Unicorn Princesses

BLOOM'S BALL

Emily Bliss

illustrated by Sydney Hanson

BLOOMSBURY

NEW YORK   LONDON   OXFORD   NEW DELHI   SYDNEY

First published in the United States of America in December 2017
by Bloomsbury Children's Books
www.bloomsbury.com

Bloomsbury is a registered trademark of Bloomsbury Publishing Plc

For information about permission to reproduce selections from this book, write to
Permissions, Bloomsbury Children's Books, 1385 Broadway, New York, NY 10018
Bloomsbury books may be purchased for business or promotional use.
For information on bulk purchases please contact Macmillan Corporate and
Premium Sales Department at specialmarkets@macmillan.com

Library of Congress Cataloging-in-Publication Data
Names: Bliss, Emily, author. | Hanson, Sydney, illustrator.
Title: Bloom's ball / by Emily Bliss ; illustrated by Sydney Hanson.
Description: New York : Bloomsbury, 2017. | Series: Unicorn princesses ; 3
Summary: Unicorn Princess Bloom asks the human girl Cressida to help with final
preparations for her birthday party, but when they discover quails destroying the
party decorations and realize that the invitation to Princess Bloom's best friend has
gone astray, they fear the celebration will be ruined.
Identifiers: LCCN 2017010910 (print) | LCCN 2017033147 (e-book)
ISBN 978-1-68119-334-2 (paperback) • ISBN 978-1-68119-333-5 (hardcover)
ISBN 978-1-68119-335-9 (e-book)
Subjects: | CYAC: Birthdays—Fiction. | Parties—Fiction. | Unicorns—Fiction. |
Princesses—Fiction. | Magic—Fiction. | Fantasy.
Classification: LCC PZ7.1.B633 Bl 2017 (print) |
LCC PZ7.1.B633 (e-book) | DDC [Fic]—dc23
LC record available at https://lccn.loc.gov/2017010910

Book design by Jessie Gang
Typeset by Westchester Publishing Services
Printed and bound in the U.S.A. by Berryville Graphics Inc., Berryville, Virginia
8 10 9 7 (paperback)
2 4 6 8 10 9 7 5 3 1 (hardcover)

All papers used by Bloomsbury Publishing, Inc., are natural, recyclable products
made from wood grown in well-managed forests. The manufacturing processes
conform to the environmental regulations of the country of origin.

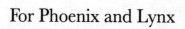

For Phoenix and Lynx

Chapter One

In the top tower of Spiral Palace, Ernest, a wizard-lizard wearing a purple pointy hat and a matching cape, put three apricots on a chair. Above him, two tomatoes, each with bright yellow wings, swooped down from a bookshelf. Near the window, three silver-winged bananas hovered. A flock of plums fluttered their gold wings around a chandelier.

Ernest cleared his throat and raised his wand. But as he opened his mouth to begin casting a spell, he heard a knock on the door. "Come in!" he called out.

The door opened, and in stepped Princess Bloom, a mint-green unicorn with a magic emerald that hung around her neck on a purple ribbon. In her mouth, she carried a blue velvet bag. Bloom smiled as she admired Ernest's flying tomatoes, bananas, and plums. Then she dropped the bag between her shiny green hooves and said, "You sure have been working hard on your flying spells. It looks like you've finally gotten the hang of it."

Ernest blushed. "I've been practicing for weeks," he said. "At the beginning, all the fruits and vegetables grew springs instead of wings. There were oranges and peaches bouncing and boinging all over the room. But now they sprout wings, usually on my first or second try."

Just then, a swooping tomato collided with a plum right above Ernest's head. With a *splat*, the tomato landed on the pointed tip of Ernest's hat. "Not again," he groaned as red juice dripped into his eyes.

Bloom giggled.

"Anyway," Ernest said, wiping his face with his cape, "what brings you to my tower?"

"I was wondering," Bloom said, "if you might use your magic to help me."

Ernest grinned with delight. The unicorn princesses often teased him about his spells, which usually seemed to go wrong. It was unusual for a creature in the Rainbow Realm to ask for his magical assistance. "I'd be most honored," he said, dabbing a final drop of tomato juice from his long, green nose.

Bloom opened the velvet bag and pulled out a stack of lime-colored, glittery envelopes. "These are invitations to my birthday party this afternoon," she explained. "I'm about to take them to the mail-snails to deliver. But there's one invitation I wanted to send in a special way." Bloom passed an

especially glittery envelope to Ernest. On
the front, it said,

To My Sister and Best Friend,
Princess Prism

"As you know," Bloom continued, "Prism
likes anything that's playful and creative.
And she loves surprises. I was wondering
if you could cast a spell on the invitation so
it grows wings and flies to her."

"Absolutely!" Ernest exclaimed, jumping up and down. "And I know exactly
which spell to use. It's in my favorite book,
Wings on Things, volume three. Or is it volume two?" Ernest scratched his forehead.

A look of concern crossed Bloom's face. "Are you absolutely sure you can do it?"

"Oh yes!" Ernest said. "I promise I won't make any mistakes."

"In that case," said Bloom, "thank you so much for your help. And now I'd better hurry to take the rest of the invitations to the mail-snails. If I don't drop them off now, the mail-snails won't have enough time to deliver them before the party starts." She smiled sheepishly. "You know me! I have trouble doing almost anything before the last minute." With that, Bloom pushed the rest of the envelopes back into the velvet bag, grabbed the sack in her mouth, and rushed out the door.

As soon as Bloom was gone, Ernest raced over to a bookshelf and pulled down a thick, black book. He flipped through the pages and stopped on page 147. Rubbing his scaly hands together, he exclaimed, "Bloom and Prism will love this!"

He put Prism's invitation on the table. He picked up his wand. And he chanted, "Happety Bappety Birthday Bloom! Wingety Swingety Fluttery Sloom! Glittery Flittery Slittery Sail! Prettily Flittery Slittery Quail!"

Ernest waited. Nothing happened. The envelope didn't even jump or tremble, and there certainly weren't any wings—or even springs—growing from it.

"Oh dear!" Ernest said, hitting his forehead with his palm. "Did I say 'quail' instead of 'mail'? Oh dear!"

Just then, thunder rumbled, and Ernest sprinted to the window in time to see several bolts of purple light flashing in the distance.

"Not again," Ernest groaned. "Hopefully, nothing will go wrong until after Bloom's party."

He shrugged and returned to the envelope. He checked the book again. And then he waved his wand and chanted, "Happety Bappety Birthday Bloom! Wingety Swingety Fluttery Sloom! Glittery Flittery Slittery Sail! Prettily Flittery Slittery Mail!" This time, the invitation spun around and two tiny, sparkling green wings sprouted from one of its corners. "Oh dear," Ernest said. "Those wings are awfully small."

The envelope flapped its wings and rose a few inches into the air. "Well, at least it can fly," Ernest said, shrugging. He carried the envelope to the open window. "Off you go to Princess Prism," he said. The envelope jumped off his hand and began to flutter, ever so slowly, down the side of Spiral Palace.

Chapter Two

Cressida Jenkins sat at her family's kitchen table with a pink pen and a stack of cards, each with a picture of a unicorn leaping over a rainbow on the front. She was writing thank-you notes to her friends who had come to her birthday celebration that past weekend. Her party had been wonderful: there had been unicorn-shaped balloons, unicorn cupcakes, a unicorn piñata, and a game of pin-the-tail-on-the-unicorn. Her friends had given her two stuffed unicorns, unicorn socks, a unicorn poster, a unicorn board game, four books about unicorns that weren't in her school's library, and a unicorn necklace.

Cressida decided to write her first thank-you note to her friend Daphne, who had given her the necklace. She wrote, "Dear Daphne," inside one of the cards. She wanted to mention, in her note, how much she loved the color of the unicorn charm, but she suddenly couldn't remember whether it was silver or gold. She was almost positive it was gold, but she wanted to check. Cressida got up from her chair and dashed down the hall to her room. She

found the necklace dangling from one of the hooks in her closet. Sure enough, a gold unicorn hung from a rainbow ribbon. She smiled, thinking about Daphne, who had a matching one. She picked up the necklace and put it around her neck. Maybe she and Daphne were now wearing their unicorn necklaces at the same time!

Just as Cressida was about to return to the kitchen, she heard a tinkling noise, like something between a harp and one of the triangles she played in music class at school. Cressida's heart skipped a beat, and an enormous smile spread across her face. She bounded over to her bedside table, opened the drawer, and pulled out an old-fashioned key with a crystal ball for a handle. The handle glowed bright pink and pulsed. The unicorn princesses were inviting her to the Rainbow Realm!

Cressida had first visited the Rainbow Realm and met the unicorn princesses after she found a similar key—old-fashioned, with a crystal-ball handle—on a walk through the woods with her parents and her older brother, Corey. Later, worried the key's owner might be looking for it, she returned it to the forest to discover the key belonged to a yellow unicorn named Princess Sunbeam. Cressida traveled with Sunbeam back to the Rainbow Realm, an enchanted world ruled by seven royal unicorn sisters. There, Cressida met all six of Sunbeam's siblings: silver Princess

Flash, green Princess Bloom, purple Princess Prism, black Princess Moon, blue Princess Breeze, and orange Princess Firefly. Each unicorn princess ruled over her own domain within the Rainbow Realm and wore a gemstone necklace that gave her unique magic powers. Cressida became such good friends with the unicorns that they gave her a key of her own. They told her she was welcome to visit any time, and that if they ever wanted to invite her back for a special occasion, the key's handle would glow bright pink.

Now, Cressida put the glowing, tinkling key in her jeans pocket. She slid her feet into her silver unicorn sneakers, which had pink lights that blinked every time she walked, ran, or jumped. She hurried into the kitchen, where she ate a blueberry granola bar in three big bites and gulped down a glass of water. Then, she called out to her mother, who was working at her computer in the living room, "I'm going for a quick walk in the woods."

"Okay, honey. Just make sure you finish your thank-you notes today," her mother called back.

"I promise I will," Cressida said. "I'll be back soon." Time in the human world froze while Cressida was in the Rainbow Realm, so she really would be back soon, even if she spent hours with the unicorns.

Cressida ran through her family's small backyard and into the woods behind her house. She raced down her favorite path, her sneakers blinking, until she came to a gigantic oak tree. She kneeled next to the tree and pushed her key into the tiny hole near the roots. Cressida grinned, giddy with excitement, as the forest began to spin, first becoming a blur of green and brown and then turning pitch black. Cressida suddenly felt as though she were falling through space, and she smiled, knowing that in a few seconds she would see the unicorn princesses.

With a gentle *thud*, Cressida landed on something soft. At first, all she could see was a swirl of silver, white, pink, and purple. But soon the room stopped spinning, and she found herself on an enormous lavender armchair. Crystal chandeliers hung from the ceilings. The scents of vanilla and cedar floated in the air. Pink and purple velvet curtains blew in the breeze. Cressida smiled. She was in the front room of Spiral Palace, the unicorn princesses' giant, shimmering, horn-shaped home.

Chapter Three

Cressida heard the clatter of hooves on the tile floors. And then, in front of her stood all seven unicorn princesses. The magic gemstones on their necklaces glittered in the light of the chandeliers.

"My human girl is back!" called out Sunbeam. She twirled and then jumped into the air, clicking her gold hooves together.

Flash flicked her mane and grinned.

Prism swished her tail and winked at Cressida.

"Welcome back, Cressida," said Breeze, Firefly, and Moon in unison.

Bloom trotted up to Cressida and gushed, "Thank you so much for coming! I was hoping you'd be able to make the trip to the Rainbow Realm this afternoon."

"Bloom insisted we invite you here," Sunbeam explained, "but she wouldn't tell us why."

"She says it's a surprise," Flash added.

"Bloom's my best friend, and she won't even tell me what the surprise is!" Prism said.

"But whatever it is," Moon added, "we're thrilled you're here."

"I couldn't be happier to be here," Cressida said. "I can't wait to find out about Bloom's surprise."

Just then, Cressida heard a high-pitched sound. She turned toward the palace door to see a teal chipmunk wearing a red uniform and blowing into a bugle. Behind the chipmunk were six giant orange snails, and attached to each enormous snail shell was a green, glittery envelope. The snails' antennae twitched as they fanned out across the room, and Cressida noticed a snail was headed straight toward each of the unicorns except Bloom and Prism. And then, to her delight, Cressida realized one snail was gliding toward her!

The snail stopped in front of Cressida and said, in a squeaky voice, "Cressida Jenkins, I presume?"

"That's me!"

"I've got a special snail-mail delivery for you," the snail squeaked.

"Thank you," Cressida said, carefully pulling the glittery green envelope off the snail's shell. She read these words, in lime-green writing, on the front:

To: Cressida Jenkins,
My Favorite Human Girl
From: Princess Bloom

The snail winked at Cressida, twirled her antennae, and slid away. Cressida opened the envelope and pulled out a card with an orange flower on the front. Inside, it read:

You are cordially invited to a
Birthday Garden Ball
for Princess Bloom this afternoon
in the Enchanted Garden.

Cressida's heart swelled with excitement. She wasn't completely sure what a garden ball was, but any kind of birthday celebration with real unicorns sounded even more fun than her own birthday party had been.

Cressida looked up to see Flash, Sunbeam, Breeze, Moon, and Firefly opening their cards. But Prism, who hadn't received one, frowned as she watched the fleet of mail-snails gliding out of the palace. Cressida wondered why Prism hadn't gotten an invitation, especially since Prism and Bloom were best friends. She couldn't imagine Bloom would exclude Prism, and she hoped a mail-snail with a card for Prism would arrive soon.

Bloom bounded over to Cressida. "Surprise!" the unicorn sang out. "The reason I invited you to the Rainbow Realm was so you could join me for my birthday garden ball. So, can you come?"

"Absolutely!" said Cressida. "I can't wait! But I have one question: What, exactly, is a garden ball?"

"I was wondering the same thing," Sun-beam said.

"Me too," Flash and Firefly said at once.

"Well," began Bloom, smiling proudly, "it's a special kind of party I made up! I love garden parties because they're outside, there's always good food, and they're not too formal. But there's never enough dancing! And I love balls because there's lots of dancing. But, to be honest, I don't always like wearing a scratchy, formal cape for hours on end. And I usually spend the whole ball feeling a little hungry because there's never very much food. So I thought I'd celebrate my birthday with the best parts of each and call it a garden ball. It will be outside with amazing food and lots of dancing. But no formal capes are allowed!"

"A garden ball," Breeze said. "What a great idea."

"That's a perfect kind of party for you," Moon said.

Cressida jumped up and down with excitement. And then she looked down at her clothes. The left knee of her jeans was torn from a time she had tripped while playing freeze-tag in the backyard with Corey. And, even worse, the front of her green T-shirt had a stain that looked like it was either from spaghetti sauce or red paint. The only thing she was wearing that looked even remotely appropriate for any kind of party was the unicorn necklace

Daphne had given her. "I'm not dressed for a garden ball," Cressida said, frowning.

"I'll fix that!" called out a high, nasal voice. Ernest jogged into the room clutching his wand.

"Hello, Ernest," Cressida said.

"I've been working on this spell for the past hour," Ernest announced, breathless. "Watch this!" He waved his wand and chanted, "Pinkery Puffery Dressery Droo! Dottily Spottily Puffily Foo!"

Wind swirled around Cressida. Then, suddenly, she was wearing a bright pink dress with white polka dots and the puffiest skirt she had ever seen. On her feet were black, shiny Mary Jane shoes. "Well?" Ernest asked excitedly. "What do you think?"

The dress felt stiff and itchy. And the shoes pinched Cressida's toes and seemed much too uncomfortable for running and jumping. Cressida decided to be honest. "It was very thoughtful of you to make this dress and these shoes for me," she said. "But they're not exactly my style."

"That's true," said Ernest, nodding. "Honestly, I'm just excited the dress came out with dots instead of pots. A dress with metal pots all over it is heavy. And noisy, too, with all that clanging. Let me try another one!"

Cressida laughed and tried not to scratch her legs, which felt itchier and itchier the longer she wore the dress's puffy skirt.

Ernest cleared his throat. He lifted his wand. And he chanted, "Greenily Sparkily

Lemmings Loo! Birthday Dressily Purple Ploo!"

Cressida felt another rush of wind. When she looked down, she was wearing purple sneakers and a bright purple party dress that was exactly right for her: it had big pockets, and it was comfortable enough for running, jumping, climbing, and dancing. But now she was back to wearing her torn jeans underneath the dress. And at her feet sat what looked like five green, glittery rodents.

"Are those mice?" Cressida asked, taking a step backward. She was pleased to notice her new sneakers had green lights that blinked when she stepped.

One of the little animals looked up and rolled her eyes. "Everyone always thinks we're mice. But we're *lemmings*. L-E-M-M-I-N-G-S! We're rodents that live in very cold places, like the Arctic. And, I must say, we usually don't look like we've been to a Saint Patrick's Day parade! In fact," the lemming sniffed, "we lemmings have refused to celebrate Saint Patrick's Day ever since a leprechaun had the nerve to call us rats!"

"Oh dear!" Ernest said. "Did I say *lemmings* again? I meant *leggings*. Let me fix that!"

Cressida giggled as Ernest waved his wand and chanted, "Greenily Sparkily Leggings Loo! Send the Lemmings Back Home, Too!"

In one last burst of wind, the lemmings vanished. When Cressida looked down, green, glittery leggings had replaced her jeans. "Thanks so much, Ernest!" she said, spinning around. "This is perfect!" She touched her hand to her chest, and, to her relief, her unicorn necklace was still there, under her dress.

Ernest blushed and took a bow.

"What a great outfit," said Bloom. "And now that you're perfectly dressed for a garden ball, want to come with me to the Enchanted Garden to help me finish getting ready?"

"I'd love to!" replied Cressida.

Just then, Sunbeam looked at Bloom and smiled teasingly. "It's just like you to send out your invitations on the very same day as your party! How did you know we wouldn't already have other plans this afternoon?"

"We love our sister Bloom, but she always does everything at the very last minute," Flash explained to Cressida. "And sometimes she even does things *after* the last minute. There was one year when she held her party after her actual birthday because she couldn't get ready in time."

Prism swished her tail and frowned. She looked like she wanted to defend her best friend, but she wasn't sure what to say, given that she still hadn't received an invitation.

Bloom smiled, but Cressida could see the unicorn felt hurt. "Sure, I should have sent out the invitations earlier," Bloom said. "But wait until you see the garden ball I have planned!"

"Planned? I'll believe that when I see it!" Sunbeam said. "But seriously, Bloom, we're all thrilled to come to your garden ball. Luckily, my only plans this afternoon were to sunbathe and to roll around in a patch of purple clover in the Glitter Canyon. I can most certainly reschedule that for tomorrow afternoon."

"Cressida is coming with me to the Enchanted Garden to finish getting ready for the garden ball," Bloom said. "We'll see you in just two hours." Then she kneeled, and Cressida climbed onto the unicorn's back. She held onto Bloom's mane, wavy and shiny like Easter-basket grass, and the unicorn turned and trotted toward the door.

Just then, Cressida heard Firefly say, "Don't worry, Prism. I bet the mail-snail delivering your invitation just took an extra-long lunch break or had to stop at the shell repair shop. I'm sure your invitation will be here in no time."

Chapter Four

Cressida felt giddy with excitement as she rode Bloom out of Spiral Palace and along the clear stones that led into the surrounding forest. She couldn't wait to see the Enchanted Garden or to celebrate Bloom's birthday.

"My sisters always tease me about waiting until the last minute," Bloom said as she came to a cluster of pine trees and turned left onto a wide, flat path. "But guess what? I've been planning this party for weeks. I've already baked a clover cake, churned dandelion ice cream, and grown a huge harvest of fruit just for the occasion. This morning, the orchard gnomes helped me blow up balloons and hang streamers. The only thing left to do is make the goody bags. And I was thinking you could help me since you have hands instead of hooves."

"Wow! Your garden ball sounds great," Cressida said, hoping she would get to meet the orchard gnomes. "And I'd be glad to help with the goody bags. Having hands is, well, awfully handy sometimes."

Bloom giggled at Cressida's joke. "I know my sisters aren't expecting a very good party. I can't wait to see their faces when they see the cake, the ice cream, and all the decorations. It's true I should have sent those invitations out earlier. But every time I was about to address the envelopes, I got distracted by something that sounded more fun. Especially since I have to use my mouth to hold the pen when I write. It takes forever!"

Just then, Bloom stopped in front of a patch of bright red mushrooms with white spots. "Speaking of fun, it will only take a few minutes to make the goody bags. I think there's time to play before we get to work."

"Sounds good!" Cressida said. Bloom kneeled, and Cressida slid onto the ground.

"I'll show you one of my favorite things to do," Bloom said. "I can't pass this mushroom patch without having a little fun, even when I'm running late."

Bloom pointed her shiny green horn at the mushrooms. The emerald on her necklace twinkled. And then, a beam of sparkling green light shot out from her horn. Immediately, the mushrooms began to grow and grow. Soon, they were twice as tall as Cressida, and they filled a space three times as large as her bedroom. For a moment, Bloom paused and admired her work. Then, she pointed her horn at three of the giant mushrooms and shrank them, one by one, so the first was Cressida's height, the second came up to her waist, and the third reached her knees. They looked, Cressida thought, like a staircase.

Bloom turned to Cressida and grinned. "Ready?" she asked. And then, before Cressida could respond, she bounded up the mushroom staircase and began to jump, soaring higher and higher into the sky. Bloom had just created the biggest trampoline Cressida had ever seen.

Cressida followed Bloom up the staircase. At the top, she smiled at the huge, spongy, red floor with white spots before she stepped to the center of the mushroom trampoline and jumped. "Wheeee!" she called out as she flew into the air. The trampoline was even bouncier than the one in Daphne's backyard.

"I told you this would be fun!" Bloom called out, hopping toward Cressida and launching herself into the air.

Cressida and Bloom squealed as they jumped and jumped, each time soaring higher and higher.

"Watch this!" Bloom said. "I've been practicing this trick for the past few months!" Then, on a particularly high bounce, Bloom somersaulted and landed on her hooves.

"Wow!" Cressida said, clapping.

"You try it!" Bloom sang out as she did two more flips in the air.

Cressida bent her knees and jumped as high as she could. She bounced three more times, each time flying higher and higher.

And then, on her fifth jump, she tucked her knees to her chest and somersaulted. To her amazement, she landed on her feet.

"Well done!" Bloom said. "I'd give that a perfect ten!"

"Thank you!" Cressida said, giggling. She took a bow.

Cressida and Bloom both did several more somersaults before Bloom said, "Do you think we should head to the Enchanted Garden? I could stay here all day, but my sisters will make fun of me if we're still putting together the goody bags when they arrive."

"Sure," Cressida said. She didn't feel like getting off the trampoline, but she wanted to make sure Bloom was ready for her garden ball before her guests arrived.

"I'm going to do one more flip!" Bloom said. "Well, actually two. I'm going to make this one a double!" And then she soared up into the air, did two somersaults, and landed on her back hooves.

"Amazing!" Cressida said.

"Do you think there's time to do just a few more somersaults?" Bloom asked.

Cressida giggled at her friend. She could see exactly how Bloom had earned her reputation for waiting until the last minute. "I have an idea," Cressida said. "How about if we go to the Enchanted Garden now, put together your goody bags, and make sure everything is completely ready. And if we finish before it's time for your garden ball, we can come back and jump some more."

Bloom nodded. "Sounds like a plan."

Bloom bounded over to the mushroom staircase, hopped down, and waited as Cressida followed her to the ground. The earth under Cressida's feet felt strangely hard and solid compared to the mushroom trampoline.

Bloom pointed her horn at the mushrooms and said, "Move out of the way! I don't want to accidentally shrink you."

Cressida quickly stepped backward as Bloom shot a green, glittery beam of light at the mushrooms until they shrank to their normal size.

"You know," said Bloom, winking, "I was just teasing about shrinking you. My magic works on objects and plants, but not on other animals." The unicorn kneeled down so Cressida could climb onto her back.

"I can't wait to see the Enchanted Garden," Cressida said.

"We're almost there," Bloom said, and she took a sharp right onto a narrow path that ended at a tall, white stone wall with an iron gate. At the top of the gate were the words, "Enchanted Garden," written in emeralds.

"Close your eyes!" Bloom called out. Cressida shut her eyes. She heard the gate open, and she felt Bloom take several steps forward. "All righty!" said Bloom. "Now you can look!"

Chapter Five

Cressida opened her eyes to see rows and rows of trees, all with leaves that looked like pieces of emerald-colored foil. "Welcome to the orchard," Bloom said as she kneeled, and Cressida slid onto the ground. "This is where I grow all the fruit my sisters and I eat."

Hanging from the branches were fruits in every color and shape Cressida could imagine. Some were fruits she recognized from the human world: apples, oranges, peaches, plums, apricots, and nectarines. She also spotted several purple-and-pink-striped roinkleberries, the sweet fruit she had eaten during her first visit to the Rainbow Realm. But most of the branches were covered in fruit she had never seen before. Shiny orange-and-blue-striped fruit cascaded in bunches like giant grapes. Red fruit with yellow spots, and yellow fruit with red spots, dangled on long, thick stems. Pink and purple fruit that looked like glittery rubber balls dotted some of the branches.

And bunches of teal, banana-like fruit swayed in the light breeze. Most of the trees held elaborate wooden birdhouses, each with several floors and entrances. Tiny bluebirds flew in and out of them, swooping from tree to tree.

Cressida noticed that nearly everywhere she looked, there were garden gnomes wearing pointy red hats and brown work boots. They were climbing up and down ladders as they filled small wooden baskets with picked fruit. They were watering the trees with purple garden hoses. And they were busily working with hammers and nails to build ladders, fruit baskets, birdhouses, benches, tables, and chairs.

"Are those the orchard gnomes?" Cressida asked. She tried not to stare, though she couldn't help herself.

"They sure are," Bloom said. "They love to garden. They pick all the fruit, water and prune the trees, and take care of the birds. Another thing about gnomes is they love building things out of wood. They spend all their spare time making furniture."

Just then, two gnomes marched over to Cressida and Bloom carrying a wooden basket. "Salutations!" they said in unison. "My name is Gnorbert," one of them said, "and this is Gnatasha."

"It's a pleasure to meet you," Cressida said, bending over to shake the gnomes' hands. "I'm Cressida Jenkins. I'm here for Bloom's birthday garden ball."

"Splendid!" the gnomes said.

"We were wondering if you might like to try some fruit," Gnatasha explained. "Nearly all the ripe fruit is already in troughs for Bloom's party. But I happen to have right here a fresh cranglenapple." She handed Cressida a shiny red fruit with yellow spots. "And this froyanana is perfectly ripe." She gave Cressida one of the teal bananas.

"Thank you!" Cressida said.

"You're most welcome," said Gnorbert. "We'd better get back to work. We're about to build a brand new bench."

"And a huge castle for the bluebirds," Gnatasha added, pulling a small hammer from her tool belt and twirling it in her fingers. The two gnomes marched off, whistling.

Bloom glanced at Cressida. "Which are you going to eat first?"

Cressida looked at the two fruits, and her stomach growled. She decided to start with the cranglenapple. She took a bite of the red-and-yellow fruit, and laughed as pink juice dripped down her chin. It tasted like a mix of watermelon, cotton candy, and mint bubble gum. "This is really good!" she said, taking several more bites to finish the cranglenapple.

"They're my second favorite," confessed Bloom. "What I really love are froyananas."

Cressida unpeeled the froyanana to find inside what looked like a magenta banana with violet stripes. Bloom smiled. "I could eat those all day long."

Cressida took a bite, and tried not to gag. It tasted like combination of pickles, marshmallows, tomatoes, and tuna fish. "I don't think this one is for me," she said, wishing she could drink some water to get the terrible taste out of her mouth.

"I'll finish it for you!" Bloom said, and ate the rest in one bite. "This one is awfully mild. Want me to see if the gnomes can find one with a stronger flavor? Maybe then you'd like it more."

"Um, no, thank you," Cressida said quickly. "I've had enough froyanana for now. I'm really not hungry anymore."

"Maybe later," Bloom suggested.

"Maybe," Cressida said, though she was quite certain she would not. She decided she would rather eat three bowls of lima beans and frozen peas—her two least favorite foods—than one more bite of froyanana.

Bloom shrugged. "Come this way, and I'll show you the vegetables," she said. Cressida followed Bloom along a row of plum trees, through a cluster of trees with ruby-red fruit the size of soccer balls, and around five gnomes building a miniature Spiral Palace for the bluebirds.

On the far side of the orchard, Bloom led Cressida through a gated wooden fence and into a vegetable garden that was the size of three classrooms at Cressida's elementary school. There were rows of plants Cressida knew from her school's garden—carrots, corn, eggplant, zucchini, tomatoes, peppers, pumpkins, yellow squash, and sugar snap peas. And then there were vegetables Cressida had never seen: purple vines with teal vegetables that looked like starfish, stout pink plants with yellow berries, and red bushes covered in white-and-black, bagel-shaped vegetables. But the strangest thing Cressida noticed were piles of small yellow dragons, each with a set of folded wings, sleeping among the vegetables.

"What are those?" Cressida said.

"Those are the mini-dragons," Bloom explained. "They're the sleepiest creatures in the Rainbow Realm." Just then, several lizards, asleep in a nearby pile, stirred and then began to snore. "The only way to

get them to wake up is to show them something metal and shiny. They love silver and gold. But other than that, forget it! They just nap all day long."

Bloom noticed a cluster of weeds by her front hooves. She pointed her horn downward. The magic emerald on her necklace glittered before she shot a green beam of light at the weeds. Almost instantly, they shrank until they were so small Cressida couldn't see them.

"I'll do more weeding later," Bloom said. "Right now, we'd better head over to the flower garden to finish making those goody bags. I can't wait to show you the cake, the ice cream, the troughs of fruit, and all the decorations. This is going to be the best birthday party my sisters have ever seen."

Bloom led Cressida to the far side of the vegetable patch, where they came to a high stone wall with a wooden gate. "Get ready!" Bloom said, and she pushed open the gate with her hoof.

Chapter Six

As soon as Bloom opened the gate, she gasped. In the walled-off flower garden, perched on the sides of all the gold and silver troughs of fruit, clustered on the wooden benches, strutting along the brick paths, and digging through the flower beds, were orange quail with lime-green eyes. Quail nibbled on Bloom's five-tiered, green and yellow cake, eating the frosting and chewing on the candles. Quail pecked hungrily at the light-green ice cream in silver buckets. Quail clustered around two large harps, using their beaks and talons to yank on the strings until they snapped in two. Quail wrapped themselves in streamers and popped balloons. A few quail even wore birthday hats. All the while, the quail excitedly repeated, "*Meep! Meep! Meep!*"

"Oh no!" whinnied Bloom. She looked at her ruined cake and blinked back tears. "How did this happen? Do you think I'll have to cancel my birthday party?"

Before Cressida could respond, three large purple earthworms, each the size of a small snake, wiggled out from a flower bed

and squirmed over to Bloom and Cressida. "We're sorry about the quail," one of them said.

"We tried to stop them," the second explained.

"But they wouldn't listen," said the third.

The first worm looked at Cressida and said, "My name is Wilhelmina. And this is Wallaby." She nodded toward the second worm. "And here's Worthington." She pointed her tail toward the third worm.

"I'm Cressida Jenkins," Cressida said.

"How did all these quail get here?" Bloom asked, frowning as a bird jumped from bal-loon to balloon, loudly popping each one.

"We were burrowing through the dirt, as usual," Worthington explained. "We'd found a great spot by those rosebushes. Then, all of a sudden, we heard thunder and saw purple lightning. The next thing we knew, there were quail everywhere."

"We asked them to go somewhere else," Wilhelmina said.

"We asked nicely at first. And then we were pretty rude," Wallaby added. "But instead of leaving, they um, well—" His voice trailed off.

"What Wallaby is too polite to say," Worthington explained, "is that they tried to eat us! It turns out the only food quail like more than cake, ice cream, and fruit is earthworm. We've been hiding in that bed of tulips ever since. The only reason they haven't already eaten us is, well, they aren't very smart."

Bloom sighed heavily. "Oh, I knew I shouldn't have trusted Ernest with that invitation."

"What invitation?" Cressida asked.

"I'll tell you later," said Bloom. "Right now we need to get the quail out of here before they start eating the rest of the Enchanted Garden. It's bad enough to lose everything I cooked and made and grew for my party. But it would be much worse to lose all the other fruits and vegetables. Then what would my sisters and I eat? Plus, we certainly don't want the quail to eat the earthworms!"

Bloom walked to the center of the flock of quail. She cleared her throat to get their attention, but they continued gnawing on candles, pecking at the cake, and wrapping themselves in party streamers. Two quail, perched on the side of an ice cream bucket, jumped in and covered their feathers in the cold, green dessert, squealing, *"Meep! Meep! Meep!"* Three other quail found a cluster of balloons behind a rosebush and popped them with their beaks. Then they played tug-of-war with the deflated balloons. Bloom stomped her hoof, but the quail still didn't look up. Finally, she whistled so loudly Cressida covered her ears.

"Attention all quail!" Bloom called out. "It's time for you to leave the Enchanted

Garden! Please fly over that wall immediately!" Bloom pointed with her horn to the far wall of the flower garden. Finally, the birds stopped pecking and playing. They stared at Bloom and blinked their green eyes. Several cocked their heads and tweeted, "*Meep?*" And then, to Cressida's dismay, they shrugged and carried on eating the party food and playing with the decorations.

Bloom looked at Cressida and frowned. "Can you think of any other way to get them out of here?"

Cressida scratched her head. And then, she had an idea. It was a strange idea. But she was pretty sure it would work.

"I think so," Cressida said, going over the details of her plan in her head. "Bloom, would you mind staying here and making sure the quail don't eat Wallaby, Wilhelmina, and Worthington while I ask the gnomes a question?"

Bloom nodded. "You always have the most creative ideas," she said. "I'll be right here, protecting the worms."

Cressida sprinted out of the flower garden, through the rows of vegetables, and back to the orchard. She spotted Gnorbert and Gnatasha under a tree building a bench. Cressida jogged over to them.

Gnorbert looked up at her and smiled. He had several nails in his mouth, and was holding a hammer. Gnatasha, busy measuring a piece of wood, barely glanced up as she asked, "How can we help you?"

"Well," said Cressida, realizing her request might sound strange, "I'm wondering if you could please build me a quail roost. And it would be good if it weren't very heavy."

Cressida waited for Gnatasha and Gnorbert to ask her why she would possibly want a quail roost, but Gnorbert said, "How many quail will need to roost on it?"

"Twenty. Or maybe twenty-five," Cressida said.

Gnatasha and Gnorbert nodded and said, in unison, "One lightweight, medium-size quail roost coming up!" They immediately began gathering wooden beams from nearby piles of wood and taking measurements with the rulers they kept behind their pointed ears. As Gnatasha started hammering, Gnorbert dashed into a shed and reappeared with three teetering stacks of nests made of blue straw.

In almost no time, Gnatasha and Gnorbert were standing on either side of what looked like a tall bookcase with a neat row of nests on each shelf. "Amazing!" Cressida said. "Thank you!" She tried to lift the roost, expecting it to be heavy. But she found she could easily carry it.

"How did you make this so light?" Cressida asked.

Gnatasha winked. Gnorbert said, "We gnomes are a little bit magic." And then they both bowed before they hurried back to building their bench.

Cressida carried the roost through the orchard and into the vegetable garden. She paused and surveyed the piles of sleeping mini-dragons, trying to decide which ones looked friendliest. Finally, she approached two sleeping in a ball beneath a bush covered with what looked like orange-and-pink-polka-dotted zucchini.

"Excuse me," Cressida said. "I'm sorry to bother you." One of the mini-dragons half-opened her eyes. "My name is Cressida. I'm friends with Bloom."

"I'm Drusilla," the mini-dragon said, stretching. "This is my brother Drudwyn." Drudwyn blinked and yawned.

For a moment, Drusilla and Drudwyn stared at Cressida. Then their eyelids began to droop. Cressida could tell they were about to fall back asleep.

"I'm wondering," said Cressida, "if you could do me a favor."

"Maybe," Drusilla said, looking annoyed. "Well, honestly, probably not. How long will it take?"

"I don't really like doing work," Drudwyn added. "It's much more fun to nap."

"I know you really like to sleep," Cressida said, "but I'm wondering if you could take a short break from napping. I only need help for five or ten minutes."

Drusilla and Drudwyn whispered for a few seconds. Then, Drusilla said, "Nope. Sorry."

"But," Cressida said, "you'd be helping to save the Enchanted Garden from a flock of quail."

Drusilla and Drudwyn shook their heads. "Sorry," Drudwyn said. "No can do."

Cressida's heart sank. Then she remembered Bloom had mentioned the dragons liked shiny presents. Cressida put her hand on her chest and felt the unicorn charm under her purple dress. She didn't want to give away Daphne's present. But saving the Enchanted Garden was more important than her unicorn charm.

Cressida pulled the necklace over her head and dangled it in front of the minidragons. Drusilla and Drudwyn stood up, widened their eyes, and stretched their long, yellow wings. "Well, well, well," Drusilla said, not taking her eyes off the unicorn charm. "That's awfully pretty. Can I hold it?"

"Not yet," Cressida said. "But you can have it to keep if you help me."

"It's a deal," Drusilla and Drudwyn said at once.

Relief washed over Cressida. "Follow me!" she said, and she put the unicorn necklace in her pocket, picked up the quail roost, and walked as fast as she could toward the flower garden.

Chapter Seven

Cressida returned to the flower garden to discover the quail had already finished eating Bloom's birthday cake and ice cream. A handful gathered around the nearly empty fruit troughs wearing smashed roinkleberries on their heads. Others had pushed pieces of froyananas onto their beaks so they looked like they had long, magenta-and-violet-striped noses. The rest of the quail milled around, hunting for more food. Worthington, Wilhelmina, and Wallaby nervously hid in an empty flowerpot behind Bloom.

Cressida put the quail roost down against the flower garden wall, right in front of one of the fruit troughs.

"What is that?" Bloom asked.

"A quail roost," Cressida explained.

Bloom raised her eyebrows. "A *roost*? We're trying to get the quail to leave the Enchanted Garden, not to stay and sleep here!"

Cressida smiled mysteriously. "I have a plan!" she said. Then she looked into the flowerpot at the worms. "I hate to ask you this," she said, "but could you squirm up onto that quail roost for just a few minutes?"

"But the quail will see us," Wallaby said.

"And they'll eat us," Worthington added.

"I promise to pick you up just as soon as the quail get near you," Cressida said. She wasn't sure what it would feel like to touch the worms, but she wasn't afraid of a little sliminess.

The worms whispered together. "It's a deal," Wilhelmina said.

"Great!" Cressida said. "I promise you'll be safe."

Next, she looked at Drusilla and Drud-wyn, now lying half-asleep at the foot of the quail roost. Cressida pulled the unicorn charm from her pocket and dangled it in front of the mini-dragons. They bolted upright. Drusilla grasped for the charm with her claws, but Cressida kept it out of reach. "When I say *Up!* I need you to fly with this roost over the garden wall and set it down gently in the woods surrounding the Enchanted Garden. The farther you take it from here, the better. As soon as you do that, I promise I'll give you this necklace."

The dragons nodded eagerly.

Cressida turned to Bloom. "Once all the quail are on the roost, can you keep them from jumping off while I rescue Wilhelmina, Worthington, and Wallaby?"

"Absolutely!" Bloom replied.

Cressida looked at the three worms. "Go ahead!" she said. Wilhelmina, Wallaby, and Worthington glanced nervously at each other. Then they wiggled up to the top of the quail roost. Immediately, the entire flock of quail noticed. For a moment, they all cocked their heads, stared at the worms, and blinked. Then the birds shrieked, "*Meep! Meep! Meep! Meep!*" as they charged toward the roost. Soon they began hopping onto the roost's shelves, hunting for the worms.

At just the moment when all the quail had gathered on the roost, one of the quail pecked dangerously close to the worms.

Cressida scooped up the three worms. They were cool and slimy in her hand, but she didn't mind.

At that same moment, Bloom pointed her horn at the trough that sat right in front of the roost. The emerald on her necklace glittered. And then a green stream of sparkling light shot from her horn, making the trough grow so large it created a wall that pressed it up against the roost. Now, the quail couldn't hop off.

"Perfect!" Cressida said. Then she turned to the mini-dragons. "Up!" she called out as she used her other hand to dangle the unicorn charm in front of Drusilla and Drudwyn. The mini-dragons grabbed the roost in their long, sharp claws. They extended their yellow wings. And they soared up into the sky with the roost, and all the quail on it.

Bloom let out a sigh of relief. "I was terrified they were going to eat my entire garden," she said. "Thank you, Cressida."

❖ ✳ ❖

"Yes," the worms said in unison, "thank you."

"I'm so glad I could help," Cressida said.

Just then, Drusilla and Drudwyn returned and landed in front of Cressida. Cressida sighed as she dropped the necklace Daphne had given her into Drusilla's scaly hands before the two mini-dragons scurried away. She hoped she could save up enough allowance money to buy herself a new one.

That was when Cressida heard Bloom sniffle. She turned and saw the unicorn crying as she looked at all the popped balloons, cake crumbs, puddles of melted ice cream, half-eaten pieces of fruit, and tangled streamers. There were even quite a few quail eggs Cressida hadn't noticed before.

"I'm so sad," Bloom said, "that those quail ruined my garden ball. And now my sisters will still think I'm not capable of planning ahead."

"I'm so sorry," Cressida said, and she wrapped her arms around Bloom's neck.

For a moment, Bloom nuzzled her face against Cressida's. And then she said, "Thank you so much for your help. Right now, I need to be alone for a little while. Will you do me a huge favor and run back to the palace and tell my sisters the party is canceled?"

"Of course," Cressida said. She certainly understood what it felt like to want to be alone. Once, when she hadn't won a prize at her school's science fair, she had been so disappointed that she had wanted to just lie on her bed by herself with the door closed. And another time, when her soccer team lost, she had taken a long walk in the woods by herself.

"Thank you," Bloom said, blinking back more tears. "I'll meet you at the palace soon. I just need a little time to myself first. But please don't go back to the human world without saying good-bye."

Cressida gave Bloom a final squeeze. And then she ran through the vegetable garden, jumping over a pile of sleeping mini-dragons on her way, and then through the orchard, where she waved to Gnorbert and Gnatasha. She felt terrible for Bloom, who had seemed so disappointed and sad.

But as Cressida left the Enchanted Garden's front gate and jogged along the paths leading to the palace, she had an idea: What if she could convince the other unicorns to throw a surprise party for Bloom? It was probably too late to organize another garden ball, but maybe, if they hurried, they could have the birthday celebration ready by the time Bloom returned. Filled with excitement and hope, Cressida began to sprint.

Chapter Eight

C ressida bounded along the clear stones that led to the front entrance of Spiral Palace and burst through the door. As soon as she stepped into the front hall, she heard Prism say, "I'm not going! She didn't even invite me."

All the unicorn princesses except Bloom were standing in a tight circle on the far side of the room. They hadn't heard Cressida come inside.

"I'm positive Bloom meant to invite you," Flash said. "You're her best friend. Something must have happened to your invitation."

Prism stamped her purple hoof. "How many times do I have to tell you? I'm not going."

"I'm staying here with Prism," Sunbeam said.

"Me too," Firefly and Moon said in unison.

Breeze sighed and looked at Prism. "I agree with Flash. Bloom probably dropped your invitation by mistake or accidentally gave it to an off-duty mail-snail."

"She did it on purpose," Prism said, stamping her hoof even harder. "She didn't invite me. I'm not going."

Just then, Cressida sneezed. The unicorns turned toward her.

"I hope you'll excuse us," Flash said. "We were about to leave for Bloom's birthday party, but we're having a disagreement."

"I completely understand," said Cressida, still catching her breath. "But here's the thing. The garden ball has been canceled." Cressida recounted the story of the quail that ruined Bloom's cake, ice cream, fruit, and decorations. She made sure to mention that Bloom had spent weeks planning and preparing for the garden ball.

"I was hoping we could quickly throw together a surprise party for Bloom right now. If we all hurry, we could have it ready by the time she gets back to the palace."

"Great idea!" Flash said.

Breeze nodded.

But Prism shook her head. "No way!" she snapped. "I'm not helping."

"Neither am I," Moon, Firefly, and Sunbeam said.

Cressida's heart sank. By the time she persuaded Prism, Sunbeam, Moon, and Firefly to help with the surprise party, Bloom would probably be back. Then, out of the corner of her eye, Cressida saw something green and glittery fluttering outside the far window. "Just a second!" she said. She hurried out the front door, jogged halfway around the palace, and found what she had spied through the window: an envelope with wings so tiny it could only fly very slowly. The envelope hovered a foot above her head, and Cressida jumped up and grabbed it. She turned it over and read the front:

To My Sister and Best Friend,
Princess Prism

Cressida grinned. She ran back around the palace, through the front door, and over to Prism. "Look!" she said. "Here's your invitation! It looks like Bloom wanted to have it fly to you as a surprise."

Relief, and then joy, spread over Prism's face as she read the words on front of the envelope and then looked inside. "Bloom invited me to her garden ball!" Prism cried out, jumping and dancing across the room. "And I still have my best friend!"

"I told you," said Flash.

"Prism," Cressida said, laughing as Prism spun around on one hoof, "we don't have much time before Bloom comes back. Now that you know she invited you, do you think we could throw a surprise party for her?"

"Definitely!" Prism said. "And I have a great idea! I'm going to gallop back to the Valley of Light to get the rainbow cupcakes I baked this morning and a huge vat of rainbow sherbet I have in the freezer. I was planning on serving them at my next art show, but this is a much better occasion." With that, Prism raced out the palace door.

"I still have some balloons and streamers left over from the Thunder Dash," said Flash. The Thunder Dash was a race Flash hosted every year in the Thunder Peaks. "I'll get them straight away!" She sped off, galloping so fast lightning crackled from her hooves and horn.

"I'm pretty sure I still have some purple party hats back in the Glitter Canyon from a birthday party I threw for the cacti," Sunbeam said. "I'll go find them." Sunbeam, who didn't like to run as much as her sisters, trotted out the front door.

"Here's what I'll do!" Firefly said. "I'll use my magic to create a huge swarm of fireflies. If I spend a few minutes practicing, I bet I can get them to spell out, 'Happy Birthday, Bloom!'" Firefly retreated to the back of the room and began shooting orange light from her horn. Soon, more fireflies than Cressida could count hovered above the unicorn's head.

Breeze thought for a minute. "I've got it!" she said. "I'll go back to the Windy Meadows and get a kite. Cressida, would you be willing to decorate it and write, 'Happy Birthday, Bloom!' on the kite's tail? I'll use my magic so a gust of air flies the kite just over our heads."

"Of course!" Cressida said.

Breeze smiled and hurried out the palace door.

"I know what I can do," Moon said, walking over to one of the front windows. "I'll stand here and wait for Bloom. As soon as I see her coming, I'll use my magic to make the room pitch black. That way, when she walks into the palace and everything is dark, the party will be an even bigger surprise."

👑

Soon, Prism and Flash returned with the cupcakes, the sherbet, two rolls of silver streamers, and a bag of gold balloons. As Prism arranged the cupcakes into a heart in the middle of the floor and Flash blew up balloons, Cressida scooped the rainbow sherbet into a trough and taped the streamers to the walls.

Just as Cressida finished putting up the last streamer, Breeze ran into the front hall with a kite and a bucket of markers. "Sorry

that took me so long!" Breeze exclaimed, panting. "I couldn't find the markers anywhere!"

"No problem!" Cressida said, and she quickly got to work coloring pictures of flowers, fruits, and vegetables on the kite. In bright, colorful letters, she wrote, "Happy Birthday, Bloom! Love, Flash, Sunbeam, Prism, Breeze, Firefly, Moon, and Cressida," on the kite's long tail.

"Well done!" Breeze said, admiring her artwork.

"Thanks!" Cressida said.

Just when Cressida was wondering what else she could do to help get ready for the party, Sunbeam sauntered into the palace with a stack of tall, cone-shaped hats.

Cressida giggled as she fastened a hat to each unicorn's head. Then she put a hat on her own head.

"How do I look?" Sunbeam asked, crossing her eyes to try to see her hat.

"Well," said Cressida, laughing, "to be honest, you and all your sisters look like you have two horns. Does my hat make me look like a unicorn?"

Sunbeam smiled. "Nope," she said. "You just look like a human girl wearing a ridiculous hat."

Right then, Moon called out, "Here comes Bloom! I'll make this room pitch black at the count of three. One! Two! Three!"

Chapter Nine

Suddenly, the front hall of the palace was so dark, Cressida couldn't see her hand when she held it a few inches from her face. She heard the palace door swing open.

"Why is it so dark in here?" Bloom asked, her voice unsteady. "Is everyone gone? Oh, this is the worst birthday ever."

As Bloom began to loudly sniffle, glittery, orange light shot from Firefly's horn, and a swarm of fireflies hovered in the air above her. At first, they looked like a thick cloud of glowing dots, but after a few seconds, they formed the words, "Birthday Happy, Boolm!"

"Oops," whispered Firefly. More orange light streamed from her horn, and then the fireflies spelled out, "Happy Birthday, Bloom!"

"What's going on?" Bloom asked, giggling.

Then, a beam of blue light shone from Breeze's horn. By the fireflies' light, Cressida watched as a gust of wind sent the kite into the air, far enough away from the

fireflies that it didn't disturb their birthday
message.

"Ready?" Moon whispered. "One! Two!
Three!"

Cressida and all the unicorn princesses
shouted, "Surprise!" as the lights in the
palace came back on.

For several seconds, Bloom looked at
the fireflies, the kite, the silver streamers, the
gold balloons, the rainbow cupcakes, and
the trough of ice cream. Her eyes glittered
with delight, and she blinked back tears of
happiness. "Thank you!" she said. "Thank
you so much! This is absolutely wonderful!"

"It was Cressida's idea," Prism said.
"She told us about what happened with
the quail. You must have felt disappointed

after working so hard to prepare for your garden ball in advance."

Bloom nodded. "I felt pretty awful. But I feel much better now. Also, you all look pretty funny in those hats."

Cressida rushed over to Bloom and wrapped her arms around the unicorn's neck. "Happy birthday," she whispered. Then, she fastened a hat on

Bloom's head and said, "Now you look funny, too!"

Bloom blushed. "I must say, this is the best last-minute party I've ever seen! And trust me, I'm an expert on last-minute parties." Then, Bloom turned to Prism. "Did you get your invitation? I asked Ernest to make it fly to you as a surprise. But when I saw all the quail in my flower garden, I guessed he accidentally cast the wrong spell. I've been so very worried you didn't get your invitation. I didn't want to think I didn't invite my best friend to my birthday garden ball!"

"Well, there was a bit of a mix-up," Prism said. "But Cressida found my invitation and gave it to me. Everything is fine now."

"Phew!" Bloom said.

Prism smiled. "I think it's time for a party game. Bloom, would you like to play Pony, Pony, Unicorn?"

"Yes!" exclaimed Bloom. "That's my favorite game! Come on, Cressida. You'll pick it up in no time." Bloom and the other unicorns formed a tight circle, and Cressida joined them, squeezing between Bloom and Prism.

"I'll go first," Flash said. She began to walk around the outside of the circle, poking each of her sisters with her horn and saying, "Pony!" But when she got to Sunbeam, she shouted, "Unicorn!" and bolted forward, running around the circle and taking Sunbeam's place. The game was exactly, Cressida realized, like Duck, Duck, Goose.

"Flash always chooses me because I'm the slowest runner," Sunbeam said, rolling her eyes as she began walking around the circle, poking each unicorn and saying, "Pony." Then, when she got to Cressida, she squealed, "Unicorn!" before she bolted around the circle. Cressida chased after her, but she had only gotten a quarter of the way around the circle before Sunbeam had slid into Cressida's spot between Bloom and Prism.

"I'm going to be on the outside of this circle forever," Cressida said, giggling.

"Unicorns are much faster runners than human girls."

"It's probably not really fair to play Pony, Pony, Unicorn with a human girl," Bloom said, winking at Cressida. "Let's play something else." But then she looked again at the cupcakes, and her eyes widened. "Actually, would any of you mind if we ate those cupcakes and that sherbet now? I'm starving!"

"I'm hungry, too," Prism said. And Flash, Sunbeam, Breeze, Moon, and Firefly all nodded.

The unicorns gathered around the cupcakes and the trough of rainbow sherbet. "Would you like some, Cressida?" Prism asked. "The cupcakes and the sherbet are both froyanana-flavored."

"Um, no thank you," Cressida said, trying not to gag at the memory of the froyananana she had tasted earlier that day.

Bloom winked at Cressida, and then she looked at her sisters, all enthusiastically chewing. "Can you believe Cressida doesn't like froyananas? She took a bite of one and didn't even want to finish it."

"Really?" said Sunbeam, looking surprised.

"Strange," Flash said.

"Humans are just kind of weird!" Prism said.

Cressida laughed. Then, she heard her stomach loudly rumbling. After so much jumping and running that afternoon, she had worked up quite an appetite.

"I heard that!" Bloom said, nodding toward Cressida's stomach. "I know you probably need to go home soon to eat some human food, but I'm so glad you could join me for my birthday. I was sure those quail had ruined everything. But, thanks to you, this has been my favorite birthday ever. It's been even better than a garden ball!"

"No problem," Cressida said. "I'm thrilled I could be here to celebrate with you, too." Cressida's stomach rumbled even more loudly, and Bloom giggled.

Cressida blushed. "It sounds like I'd better go home and eat a snack! Plus, my birthday party was just last week, and I told my mother I would finish writing all my thank-you cards this afternoon."

"Just promise you'll come back soon," Bloom said.

"Of course I will!" Cressida exclaimed, and she said good-bye to Bloom, Flash, Sunbeam, Prism, Breeze, Moon, and Firefly.

"Good-bye, Cressida!" the unicorns all called out. "We already can't wait for your next visit!"

Cressida plunged her hand into the pocket of her purple party dress. Sure enough, there was the key. She wrapped both hands around the crystal handle and closed her eyes. "Take me home, please!" she said.

Suddenly, the front hall of the palace began to spin, first forming a swirl of pink, white, silver, and purple before everything went pitch black. Then, Cressida felt as though she were flying straight up into the air. She smiled, thinking that the feeling of flying was her favorite part of traveling to and from the Rainbow Realm.

When the flying sensation stopped, she found herself sitting at the base of the giant oak tree. For a minute, the forest spun around her, but then it slowed to a stop. Cressida took a deep breath. She looked down. She was wearing her silver unicorn sneakers, her old jeans with the torn left knee, and her green T-shirt with the red stain on the front. And dangling around her neck on a rainbow ribbon was the unicorn charm Daphne had given her for her birthday. Cressida smiled. Then she stood up and skipped home, her sneakers blinking all the way, to have a snack and finish her thank-you notes.

DON'T MISS OUR NEXT MAGICAL ADVENTURE!

TURN THE PAGE FOR A SNEAK PEEK . . .

In the top tower of Spiral Palace, Ernest, a wizard-lizard, scratched his long nose. He straightened his pointy purple hat and his matching cape. He picked up his magic wand. And he gazed down at a gray slug staring up at him from the tabletop. She twittered her long antennae. "I've been dreaming of this moment for months," she said. "Thank you so much for helping me!"

Ernest grinned. "It's my pleasure," he said. "And besides, I've been looking for excuses to practice my color-changing spells." He cleared his throat. He lifted his wand above his head. And then he stopped. "Um," he said, blushing, "could you remind me one more time what color you want to be?"

The slug smiled. "Ever since I was a tiny girl slug, I've longed to be the color of green grass. I'm tired of looking like a storm cloud."

"I've got to admit, it is awfully nice being green," Ernest said, looking down at his scaly, green hands. "And I've got just the right spell." He raised his wand again. But then he paused and his cheeks turned an even deeper shade of pink. "Oh dear, I've already forgotten your name. Could you tell me, just one last time?"

The slug rolled her eyes. "Sally," she said. "Sally the Slug."

"Oh yes, of course. That's right," Ernest said. "Now I'm ready." He took a deep breath. And he waved his wand as he chanted, "Sluggadug Swiggadug Sludge-rug Slass! Make the Valley as Clear as Glass."

Ernest stared at the slug and waited. But her head, tail, and antennae remained gray as ever. He furrowed his brow. "Now, why didn't that work?" he asked.

Emily Bliss lives just down the street from a forest. From her living room window, she can see a big oak tree with a magic keyhole. Like Cressida Jenkins, she knows that unicorns are real.

Sydney Hanson was raised in Minnesota alongside numerous pets and brothers. She has worked for several animation shops, including Nickelodeon and Disney Interactive. In her spare time she enjoys traveling and spending time outside with her adopted brother, a Labrador retriever named Cash. She lives in Los Angeles.

www.sydwiki.tumblr.com